THE BOY, THE BOXER
and the *Yellow Rose*

THE BOY, THE BOXER
and the *Yellow Rose*

Because you're never truly lost. You're healing.

DANIELLE GROSSE

ILLUMIFY
MEDIA.COM

The Boy, the Boxer, and the Yellow Rose

Copyright © 2025 by Danielle Grosse
Illustrations copyright © 2025 by Jenna Grosse

All rights reserved. No part of this book may be reproduced in any form or by any means—whether electronic, digital, mechanical, or otherwise—without permission in writing from the publisher, except by a reviewer, who may quote brief passages in a review.

The views and opinions expressed in this book are those of the author and do not necessarily reflect the official policy or position of Illumify Media Global.

Published by
Illumify Media Global
www.IllumifyMedia.com
"Let's bring your book to life!"

Paperback ISBN: 978-1-964251-53-0

Typeset by Art Innovations (http://artinnovations.in/)
Cover design by Debbie Lewis

Printed in the United States of America

Contents

The Story Behind the Story 6

Introduction 8

Prologue 11

Part I Releasing the Hurt 15

Part II Rebuilding Trust 37

Part III Rediscovering Life 57

Part IV Risking Love Again 75

Acknowledgements 89

35 Lessons from a Mended Soul 91

About the Artist 94

About the Author 95

The Story Behind the Story

After my mother met the fiancée of her grandson (and my son), she couldn't wait to tell me her first thoughts. Standing in her backyard surrounded by colorful zinnias, she took my hand and said, "Jenna will be your friend for life."

But even my mother's foresight didn't prepare me for the journey on which I would embark with my new daughter-in-law and new friend for life.

A year ago, Jenna shyly approached me and said, "I think we can write a book together, and people will like it."

As she described her vision, the reasoning part of my brain cried out, "No! No! No! You'll have to tell her you can't do it. You have no idea how to write a fable—plus you don't even have a story in mind!"

Two days later, I told the reasoning part of my brain to quiet down.

I had the story.

As I continued developing the story—a fable about the isolation of pain and the path to healing—I was totally unprepared for what happened next.

Hiking with my husband in Colorado, I took a serious fall that resulted in three broken vertebrae, a pelvis fractured in three places, and a blood clot. Life was interrupted by pain and interventions.

As I began my long recovery, I finally returned to the story that had been taking shape in my heart and mind before my spirit and body underwent such trauma.

When I began writing the opening words to my story about the isolation of pain, I had no idea that writing this book was no longer just for my reader—the process would carry me through my own healing process. I had no idea. *But God knew.*

Let me tell you, I've wrestled, sobbed, and healed through these pages.

THE STORY BEHIND THE STORY

On the nights I couldn't speak because of the pain, I lay on the floor with my face on the carpet, praying for Jesus to rub my back. I imagined the images Jenna was creating, and each time my phone pinged with a text of her latest illustration, I felt blessed with a message that told me, "Hang on. God knows what He's doing."

I don't know what motivated you to pick up this book today. You may be hurting emotionally or physically and looking for hope. Or maybe you are praying for a gentle way to reach out to someone lost in their own world of hurt.

Whatever prompted you to step into this story, I want you to know it was written by a soul who understands deep hurt and the need to believe things will get better.

The best books don't only leave the readers changed for the better, they change the lives of the authors as well.

This little fable changed *my* life and taught me that sometimes the gentlest of stories can mend the deepest of pain, that God cares for us and sheds tears as He heals us, and that we can experience true heartache and still find our happily ever after.

May it bless you and those you share it with on your own journeys into healing.

Introduction

Are you feeling exhausted by life?

Do you long to rest, but you're not sure how?

Has striving to "fix" your situation, yourself, and your pain left you feeling like a failure and more hopeless than ever?

Perhaps in your exhaustion you've started withdrawing from life. Maybe being alone felt soothing at first, as if your heart had finally found the protection it needed, but now the walls you've built are starting to keep you away from everything you love.

Oh, friend, I've been there too. I've lived through griefs and disappointments that have left me so numb I was afraid to express my true feelings. And honestly, I began to believe that if I ever told anyone about my hopelessness, they might decide I wasn't worth saving.

Wanting to avoid being judged (and desperate to believe I had some remnant of strength and joy left in me), I set about trying to "fix" myself.

- I purchased countless self-help books. After pondering a few reflection questions (I certainly didn't have the energy to journal about them as the authors suggested), I threw the books in my nightstand drawer, berating myself with the thought, *Another unfinished project, another failure.*
- I tried Bible studies. Amazed at the faith of the women around me, I wondered why I couldn't seem to find victory. After seeing all the highlighted passages and beautifully colored margins in their Bibles, I closed my own in shame.
- I spent time on my knees. My prayer life was anemic on good days. I was in mere tears most other days.

Everything I tried didn't work. And the more I strived, the more hopeless I felt.

INTRODUCTION

I needed something simple. Something that could comfort and encourage my soul. Something that would give me rest even as it gently led me toward hope and healing.

I needed a cup of tea and a sweet story.

Maybe you need these things too. Because even when we are feeling too weary to take a class, read a how-to book, or even have coffee with a friend, we are never too exhausted for a story.

This fable is about a boy and a dog. It's a story about unexpected discoveries on an unexpected journey. Most importantly, it's a story that whispers ancient truths.

Healing doesn't usually happen all at once because of a grand epiphany. More often than not, we heal through a collection of gentle revelations. A little bit of hope goes a long way. We have choices to make—eventually deciding to let go of the past and trust in the power of love will be one of them.

And the most remarkable discovery is simply this: We can go through hard things and still find a happy ending.

So, make yourself a cup of tea, grab your favorite cozy throw, and let me tell you a story.

As you accompany a wounded dog and boy on their own healing journey, I hope your heart is encouraged and pray that no matter where you are in your story, God surrounds you and guides you through these pages.

With much love,
Dani

*For the glory of God. Without Him, we wouldn't exist.
More importantly, without Him, there would be no love
to make us whole.*

Prologue

With a "Just Married" sign still clinging to the rear window of their Jeep, the young man kills the engine, runs around the vehicle, and opens the door for his wife. She grins as she hangs onto the wriggling bundle in her arms. With a chuckle, she sets it gently on the grass in the front yard of their little brick house in the suburbs.

It runs in circles.

A brand-new puppy!

Can life get any better?

Warm brown eyes gaze at them trustingly. The little guy wags his nub of a tail. His gangly legs tangle in his leash as he navigates the front steps leading to his forever home.

Days fill with mountain sunshine and summer activities: rafting, hiking, paddle boarding. The pup does it all. But what he loves most is cuddling with his people by a campfire on the riverbank. He listens to the rhythmic sounds of the water, laughter, and meaningful conversations.

In the evenings, the puppy curls up at the foot of the couple's bed, waiting for his favorite lullaby and the man's gentle snoring, which lets the puppy know that his little family is at peace.

After several months, the reassuring sounds are replaced by worried whispers.

"How will we make it?" the woman often asks her husband. "Why didn't we see this coming?"

Lazy mornings over coffee disappear. Relentless phone alarms provide jarring starts to the day. Dishes land in the kitchen sink with a clatter. The man and woman begin coming and going, working different shifts at odd hours.

The puppy retreats under the bed, holding on to memories of what used to be.

PROLOGUE

One day the man opens the door of a dog crate. The puppy trusts him and goes inside, hoping no one will worry about him. But they don't care at all. Other than sliding food and water into the crate each morning and offering bathroom breaks, they ignore him.

Day after day, he rests his head between his paws, waiting.

One afternoon he hears the man talking on the phone. "Yeah, we bought a boxer puppy right after our honeymoon, but he's just too much for us."

And then, the puppy's worst fears are confirmed.

"Yeah, I feel bad. But with both of us working so much, we don't have time for him. Or the budget."

The puppy scoots to the far end of the crate, trying to make himself as small as possible.

It's all my fault, he thinks.

Still on the phone, the man leans down and peers into the crate. Then he releases the latch and opens the door. "Your friends want to buy a boxer?" he says into the phone.

The dog feels a lump in the pit of his stomach. His spirit teeters on the brink.

"Actually, that would be a relief. Tomorrow is great. I'll text you our address."

The dog eyes the open crate door. Instead of walking through it, he slowly turns a circle, stretches his legs, and then lies back down. There is nothing left for him outside of his cage.

The next day, miles out of town, a college boy jumps in his pickup truck. He frowns as he throws the gears into reverse. He is exasperated, frustrated, irritated.

He flips down the truck visor. *My parents and their rescues. I don't have time for a mercy mission. Why does everyone expect me to fix everything?* he says to himself.

A few hours later, he parks in front of a little brick house in the suburbs, walks up the front steps, and knocks on the door.

PART I

Releasing the Hurt

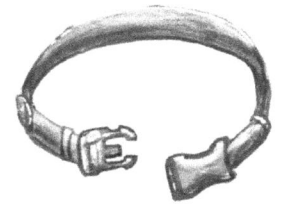

The boy stoops low. He opens the catch on the dog crate, expecting an energetic dog to bound through the door. Nothing happens.

He puts his hands on his knees and drops his head lower. "Hey, Pal," he calls.

Nothing.

He twists his baseball cap backward. "Come on, I'm taking you to a new home."

The dog hesitates. Unconvinced, he tentatively steps out of his box.

The boy strokes the dog's velvety ears. "Good job, I got you now."

His new companion quietly follows him to the pickup.

The boy opens the door and pats the front seat. "You can ride up front with me," he says.

And the young dog learned: Step by step, hope nudges us forward.

They ride in silence. The dog watches the countryside pass, mile after mile. He glances at the boy.

The boy takes one hand off the wheel and pats his knee.

The dog obeys the silent command and rests his head on the boy's thigh. The boy rubs the canine's ears.

As the pickup truck rolls down the road, the rescued dog lifts his head. He looks up at the boy with a grateful expression. Then he wags his nub of a tail and nudges the boy's hand with his nose.

"What should I name you?" the boy asks, scratching the dog's ears.

"Boxer," the dog says. "Because I had to live in a box."

"You don't live in a box now."

"But I did. It's who I am."

"That's ridiculous. It's not who you are. It's just your breed."

"Isn't that a little ironic?

The boy sighs and glances down at the dog. "You don't have to let that define you, buddy. That box isn't you. It's just part of your story."

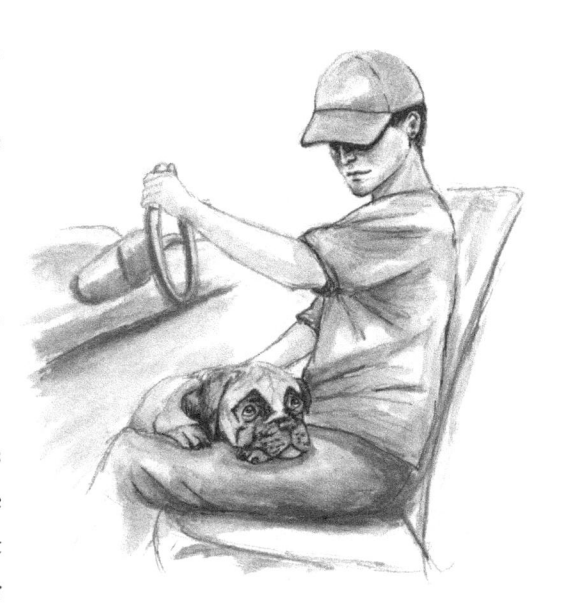

The dog settles his head back down on the boy's thigh, comforted.

> And then the young dog learned: Hard things don't change who we are, but they can make us forget for a little while.

The boy clicks the turn signal. "I need to name you something other than Boxer," he engages.

The dog looks up.

"I think I'll call you Mack-Dog. It suits you. Strong and sturdy like a truck."

The dog nuzzles the boy's leg. "I love you," the dog says.

"How can you know?" the boy asks and then smiles. "We've only been together a short time."

"When I'm with you, it feels like home."

The boy watches Mack-Dog's eyelids droop as he begins to fall asleep. He studies his passenger and feels a pang of regret. "I wish I could keep you."

The dog opens his eyes and looks quizzically at him.

The boy lifts his baseball cap and scratches his head. "My parents made a promise," he says. Mack-Dog gazes at him, and the boy continues, "My grandfather is very lonely. In a few days he's going back to Texas, and you will be going with him. He needs you."

The two ride in silence.

"But I can't help," the dog says. "I have nothing to offer. I'm just a boxer."

"His time is short. His heart is weak."

"Does he have a crate?"

"No."

"I'll go," Mack-Dog says, nuzzling the boy's ear with his wet nose. "Maybe I need him too."

"Why do you think that?"

"Maybe we can both learn how to let go of what was."

RELEASING THE HURT

As the boy and Mack-Dog pull into the driveway of a house by the river, the dog begins to tremble.

The boy turns off the engine and studies his companion. "What's up?"

Mack-Dog paws at his own nose. "Nothing."

The boy furrows his brow. "You'll like my grandfather." He opens the truck door. "Hear that? Hummingbirds. We're home."

As the dog jumps off the front seat, he listens to the buzz of the tiny birds hovering around a feeder filled with red liquid warmed by the sun.

He catches a scent of the river. He wishes he could stay here with the boy forever.

> And then Mack-Dog learned: When it comes to healing, the path forward can hold unexpected twists.

The boy races up the front porch steps, taking two at a time. Mack-Dog senses his happiness and runs right behind him. Before they reach the front door, it swings open. The boy's mother stands in the entryway, her arms open to greet them.

As the boy hugs his mama, he peers over her shoulder, spying his grandfather sitting at the dining room table. He looks at his grandson with hopeful eyes.

"He's perfect!" The boy announces. "You'll love him!"

Mack-Dog hides behind the boy, trying to find the courage to reveal himself.

The old man leans toward Mack-Dog, balanced by his cane. He smiles and pulls a treat out of his pocket. "Come on now, no need to be shy."

Mack-Dog slowly approaches his new owner. He sniffs the man's shoe.

"It's okay, Pal," The boy says. "Take the treat."

Mack-Dog gently accepts the beef-flavored morsel. Trying hard to be the perfect dog, he sits next to the elderly gentleman like a newly hired bodyguard.

Standing on the bank of the river, the boy scans the water. He casts his fishing line into the Colorado River. Hummingbirds *whir* in the background. He looks at Mack-Dog. "What do you think of my grandfather so far?"

Mack-Dog sniffs the grassy bank. "He's slow, but he's kind."

"Be careful you don't run into his cane," the boy says while reeling in his line.

The dog nuzzles the boy's knee. "He's sad."

"I know."

"He's a boxer too."

The boy gives up on the uncooperative fish. He picks up a smooth stone. "What do you mean?" he asks.

The canine looks at the rock in the boy's hand and then gazes into the afternoon sky. "He seems defeated. I think he's afraid he will be disappointed. So, he's willing to stay trapped." Mack-Dog paws at the river rock beach beneath him. "I felt like that each time the door to my dog crate opened."

The boy skims the stone across the river.

"I'll help him break out of it," Mack-Dog says.

"How?"

Mack-Dog cocks his head. "I think I'll try love and acceptance."

And then Mack-Dog learned: We often give to others what we long to receive ourselves.

RELEASING THE HURT

The next morning, the grandfather hobbles across the driveway to his motor home. He checks his pocket to make sure he remembered the dog treats. He opens the passenger door as he whistles softly.

The boy and Mack-Dog hear the whistle and come. The boy's father and mother stand on the porch. The father slips his arm around the mother's waist while she takes a sip of coffee. She peeks over the rim of her cup trying to hide her emotions.

The boy walks his four-legged friend to the motor home. He scratches the dog's ears. "Go on now, " he says.

Mack-Dog takes the last few steps on his own. He looks back at the boy one last time. He jumps in the passenger seat.

The grandfather smiles at the family on the porch. "That's some co-pilot you got me," he says. "Look at him in that front seat!"

The boy's mother calls out, "We love you!"

The boy isn't sure exactly who she's talking to, the emotionally fragile old man or the dog.

As the grandfather steers the giant motor home though sweeping turns of mountain passes, he eyes his new companion. "Would you like to hear a little bit about the love of my life?" he asks.

Mack-Dog looks out the window, watching the river disappear and the mountains fade. He turns to his new owner and solemnly nods his head.

The old man wipes his forehead with the back of his hand. "We met in Canada, picking blueberries…"

Hours pass. Mack-Dog tries to listen as his dream of living with the boy on the river fades with the setting sun.

> And then Mack-Dog learned: Even during the loneliest moments,
> love is revealed in the way we care.

Several months later, on a windy day in Colorado, a sturdy crate sits in the middle of a vast airplane hangar filled with a half dozen planes. The wind blows through the open hanger door, shaking the metal walls.

Mack-Dog presses his nose against the wire mesh of the crate. He sees the boy standing with a woman. She hands him a clipboard, and he signs his name.

Mack-Dog tentatively begins to wag his tail nub. He presses his nose harder on the mesh as the boy walks toward the crate.

He begins to whine. "He died," Mack-Dog says.

"I know."

"They put me in a crate."

The boy opens the box latch. "That's the only way I could get you home."

And then Mack-Dog learned: Sometimes the path home doesn't feel fair, even when it's taking us where we long to be.

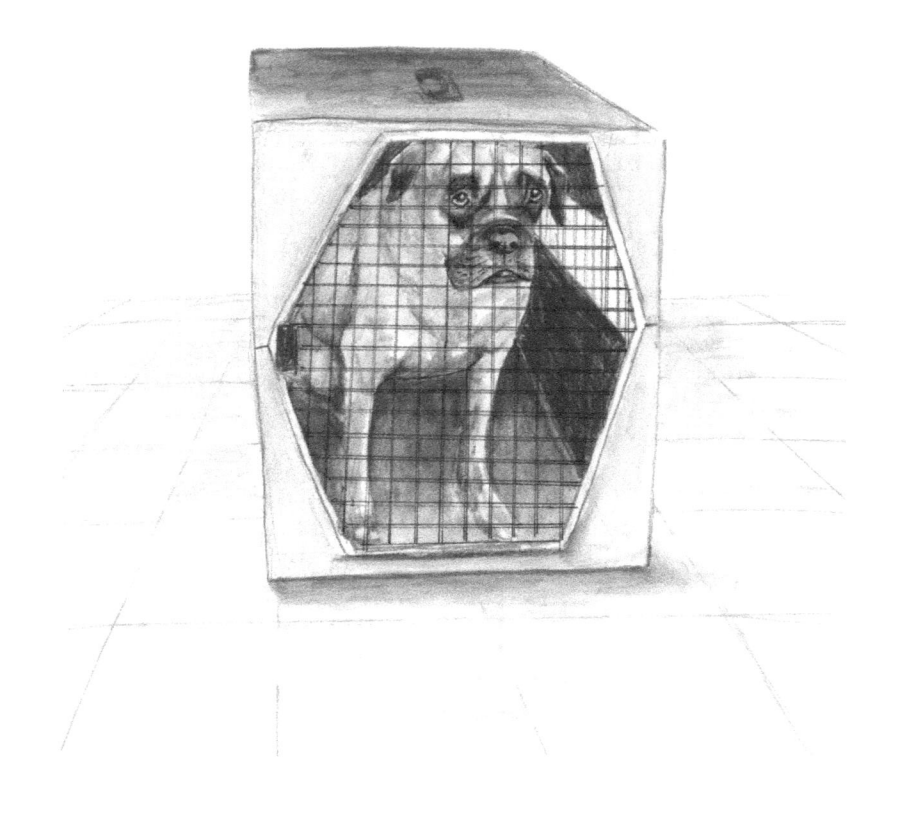

Mack-Dog turns a circle in the crate. "I'm not sure I'm ready."

"For what?"

"To be happy again."

The boy looks at Mack-Dog with a gentle expression. He reaches through the box door and pats his head softly before speaking. "Take the next step. I'll be here."

"I just peed on the floor."

"It's okay. I've still got you."

Mack-Dog eagerly jumps into the pickup truck's front seat. "Are we going to the river?" he asks.

"Not this time. We're going to my college house. You'll love it. I have roommates, and we do lots of fun stuff."

The next day, the boy and Mack-Dog stand on the porch.

The boy sips his coffee. "You chewed up my running shoes," he says.

Mack-Dog looks away.

The following day, the boy slams the door to the porch. "You ate my sunglasses."

Mack-Dog's eyes soften.

The day after that, the boy stands on the porch and tugs at his hair. "You tore up my roommate's boots."

Mack-Dog's eyes plead for forgiveness. "Do you still love me?" he asks.

"Argh, I'm going for a drive."

Mack-Dog jumps in the pickup. He puts his head on the boy's thigh. The windows are down. The radio sings.

"I'm sorry," Mack-Dog says.

The boy looks down at his dog and then stares through the windshield.

Mack-Dog looks at the boy's wallet on the seat between them. He takes it in his mouth and starts to chew.

The boy yells, "No! Drop that wallet!"

Mack-Dog tosses the wallet out the window. The boy pulls over on the side of the highway. He searches for the wallet in the weeds.

He looks at Mack-Dog and asks, "Why?"

His companion hangs his head. "I got scared," he says.

"Of what?"

"Of what might happen if you quit loving me."

The boy falls to his knees. He puts his arms around Mack-Dog's neck and buries his face in his fur.

Mack-Dog nuzzles the boy's ear.

And then Mack-Dog learned: Even when fear makes a mess of things, real love doesn't walk away.

Mack-Dog settles into his new life with ease.

In the house filled with college boys, Mack-Dog sleeps in late and soaks up the sun, enjoying the simple pleasures of life.

He has the freedom to play and explore.

The boy takes him on long runs every day.

Mack-Dog sees how the college boys let go of their worries and live in the moment. He wants to do the same. He gives himself permission to feel joy. He begins to believe that he is truly loved.

One morning the boy steps carefully over Mack-Dog sleeping on the porch. The boy is carrying a cardboard box.

Mack-Dog stirs and shakes his head from side to side. "What are you doing?" he asks.

"Taking boxes to the curb," The boy says, shifting the load in his arms.

Mack-Dog stands, slowly looking around. "Did I miss something?"

The boy looks back over his shoulder as he walks to the curb and says, "I graduated."

Mack-Dog looks concerned. "Where are we going? he asks.

The boy smiles. "Home to the river," he says.

"Why are you going home? You graduated. Don't you have all the answers now?"

"Not yet."

"But I thought you are done with school."

The boy softly chuckles. "Sometimes we need to go back to where we started to move forward."

Mack-Dog sits on his bottom and scratches his ear with his hind leg.

And then Mack-Dog learned: When we feel like we don't have all the answers, it's okay to return to a place that feels safe.

The next day, Mack-Dog takes a brave stance on the porch and barks toward the curb.

The boy rushes out the front door.

"Why is he here?" Mack-Dog asks, staring at the stranger from the street. "He smells like camping but without the marshmallows."

"We don't need those things anymore. Maybe he can use them."

"But your running shoes are in that pile."

"I know."

Mack-Dog stands firm. "You're giving your shoes away, but you were very mad at me for eating them."

"Sorry, I was angry."

Mack-Dog sniffs in the air. "I tested you," he says.

The boy kneels down and rubs his friend's ears. "Did I pass?"

The dog melts into his arms. "You loved me when I was unlovable."

And then Mack-Dog learned: Sometimes pushing a little is a way of asking, "Will you forgive me?"

That afternoon, the boy asks his roommates, "Have you seen Mack-Dog?"

When they answer no, his heart races as he runs from room to room. He checks every corner of the house and the garage. Panic sets in as he realizes the gate to the backyard is open.

He jumps into his pickup truck and throws it in reverse. Before he steps on the accelerator, a homeless man knocks on his window.

The boy rolls down his window.

The man struggles to lift the dog. "Is he yours?" he asks.

Boy almost shouts with relief, "Where did you find him?"

The man scratches Mack-Dog's ears. "McDonald's," he says.

The boy opens the truck door. "That's a long way from here. How did you know that's my dog and where I live?"

The man raises his foot, showing off his shoe. He proudly shakes it from side to side. "You gave me your shoes. I forgot to thank you for being kind."

And then Mack-Dog learned: Sometimes kindness finds its way back to us in the most unexpected ways.

The boy takes Mack-Dog on a short walk to the park. They stand on the banks of a pond, anticipating the sun's disappearance behind the mountains. He glances at his dog and asks, "Why did you leave?"

"I smelled coffee."

"But you don't drink coffee."

"I know, but you do, and I couldn't find you."

"I keep telling you not to be scared," the boy says, blowing on the steaming liquid. "I'm not going to leave here without you."

"When my first family kept me in the crate, I thought if I was good enough, they would want me." Mack-Dog twists to nervously bite at his back leg.

The boy takes a sip of hot coffee and listens.

"I'm always afraid it will happen again. I'm a Boxer, remember? The crate was my box. Now the *fear* of the crate is my box."

The boy gently traces his finger around the dog's collar, as if freeing him from something unseen. "You know, friend, it's okay to let go of the past," he says.

Mack-Dog looks up as the sky as the sun slowly dips behind the mountain.

"See that?" The boy asks, pointing to the sun disappearing beneath the horizon. He wraps his hands again around his coffee mug. His furry companion leans into him. The boy feels his warmth and continues, "The sun always comes back—just like I will."

The wrinkles around Mack-Dog's eyes relax. "You mean I don't need to pull you into my box, so I don't lose you?"

His friend grins at him and takes a sip of coffee.

And then Mack-Dog learned: Letting go feels safter when we know that a true friend will always be there for us.

RELEASING THE HURT 35

The next day, the boy rolls down the window and turns the pickup truck onto the dirt road leading to the house on the river. Minutes later, he pulls into the driveway. He cuts the engine. Mack-Dog waits for him to make the first move.

After several moments, the boy turns to him and asks, "Do you hear that?"

Mack-Dog cocks his ears from side to side.

The boy pulls his keys out of the ignition. "Hummingbirds and the river. We're home."

PART II

Rebuilding Trust

The next morning, the boy wakes up early, eager to explore the river again with his friend. He combs his fingers through his bed head, trying to calm rebellious tufts of hair. The smell of coffee directs his feet toward the kitchen.

He looks around the room for Mack-Dog. As he glances through the window, he sees a flicker of fur darting toward the river.

He goes outside to get a closer look.

The first thing he sees is a giant pile of sticks heaped on the patio. What could have made such a mess?

He scans the yard. Mack-Dog heads toward him, carrying a massive branch in his mouth.

"Mack-Dog! What do you think you're doing?"

Mack-Dog stops mid-step. He drops his stick.

REBUILDING TRUST

The next day, the boy loads Mack-Dog into his pickup truck.

Sitting obediently in the front seat, Mack-Dog asks, "Where are we going?" while giving his friend the side-eye.

The boy adjusts his rearview mirror. "A guy I know is working cattle today. I promised to give him a hand."

Mack-Dog looks out the window, unsure of what to expect.

After they arrive at the ranch, the boy leans against the fence, making plans for the day with the rancher. As they talk, Mack-Dog watches the cowboys and their dogs move the cattle from one pasture into another.

A moment later, the boy looks toward the far pasture. Mack-Dog has slipped away and joined the cow dogs. The boy shakes his head as he watches his dog nip at the heels of the calves, persuading them to file into the next field.

He adjusts his ball cap and looks at his friend.

The rancher grins. He pulls a long stem of alfalfa from between his teeth. "He shouldn't know how to do that," he says.

"And yet, watch him go!" the boy exclaims.

As the sun sets, the rancher shuts the final gate on the new pasture.

Dusty and dirty, the boy and Mack-Dog climb into the pickup truck to go home. Mack-Dog stretches across the front seat and puts his head on the boy's knee. He hopes he did good today.

A few hours later, a man pulls his car into the dark driveway in front of the house on the river. He gets his suitcase from the seat next to him. As he walks toward the front door, the motion sensor light on the side of the house announces his arrival.

The boy opens the front door.

Without warning, Mack-Dog rushes past the boy, barking furiously.

The man playfully runs toward Mack-Dog, growling and raising his hands above his head.

Frightened, Mack-Dog turns and runs off into the darkness, toward the safety of the river.

The boy whistles.

Mack-Dog lets out a hesitant, quick yelp.

The boy continues to call.

Warily, the dog appears from the shadows.

The man kneels and opens his arms. It is the boy's dad. Mack-Dog sinks into his embrace.

After the man goes into the house, Mack-Dog follows the boy to the riverbank.

The boy sits down, pulling his knees toward his chest. He reaches out and scratches the dog's hind quarter. "What was that all about?" the boy asks.

Mack-Dog adjusts his stance, encouraging the boy's scratching motion. "I thought I should protect you."

The boy half smiles, his eyes beam with quiet approval. "And how did that work for you?" he asks.

Mack-Dog grunts.

The boy stifles a laugh. He thinks about the last few days. "So what's been going on with you? The sticks, the cows, the barking?"

Mack-Dog looks deep into his eyes. "I'm trying to be the perfect dog."

Boy rubs his friend's ears. "We love you just the way you are."

And then Mack-Dog learned: We try so hard to be perfect, but real love isn't something we have to earn.

An hour later, the boy and his dog are still sitting quietly on the riverbank, lost in their own thoughts.

Mack-Dog rolls on his back, and the boy absent-mindedly scratches his stomach.

Eventually, Mack-Dog rolls over and places his muzzle under the boy's hand, demanding more attention. "I'm lost," Mack-Dog says.

The boy gently rubs Mack-Dog's velvety ears. "You're not lost; you're here with me."

"I don't want to live in a box."

"I don't even own a crate."

"Not a *real* crate. The invisible one."

"Ah."

"Without it, I'm not sure what to do. I'm not sure who I am."

And then Mack-Dog learned: We need to be patient with ourselves as we become who we really are.

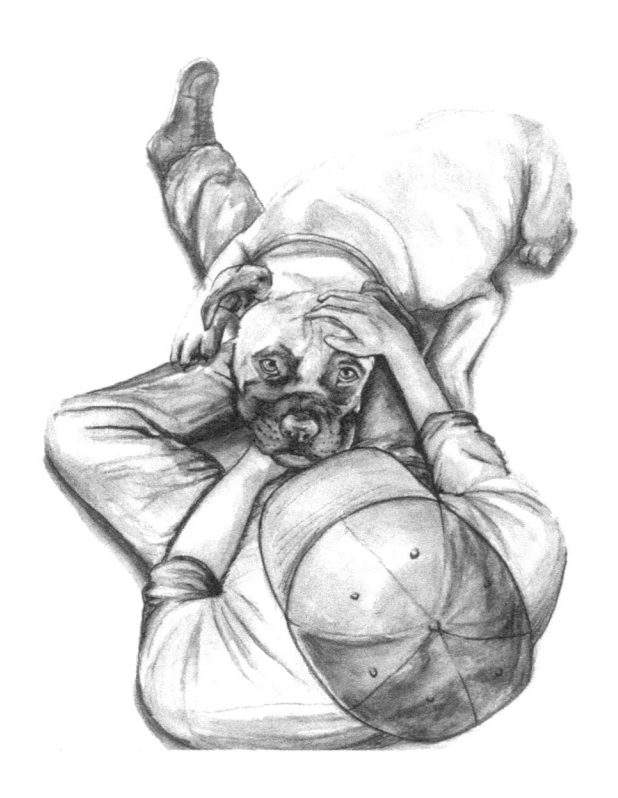

The boy stands. Turning his back on the river, he faces the mountains, dark and ominous in the night.

Mack-Dog does the same.

The boy silently scans the evening sky, filled with a treasury of sparkling lights. "Can you see the river?" he asks.

The dog cocks his ears from side to side. "No."

The boy turns around and faces the river again. Mack-Dog does the same.

"You can't look in two directions at the same time. The mountains are like your experiences in the past. The river is your future. Which way will you face?"

And then Mack-Dog learned: Stepping forward means gently releasing the past and letting hope lead.

A few nights later, the boy and his faithful companion find themselves on the bank of the river again. This time the boy carries a hammock, which he strings up between two trees.

They lie on their backs and gaze at the stars.

The boy points out constellations.

The dog watches.

Time slows.

The boy continues pointing to the vast and dark night sky above. His finger follows a path to the twinkling lights of the Big Dipper. He encourages his friend to locate the pattern of stars. "When you locate it, you will see seven bright stars that look like a ladle."

The dog lifts his chin high and scans the evening sky.

The boy moves Mack-Dog's chin in the right direction. "When I feel lost, I look in the sky and find those seven stars. They remind me that God is still in the heavens. He has everything in place."

Mack-Dog stares at the pattern illuminated in the sky. "Do you see what I see?"

The boy looks up.

The dog softly whines then says, "The three stars in the handle lead to an open box."

The boy inhales sharply. "Only you could see that, Pal." his friend's voice is filled with admiration.

They rest in the moment, not wanting it to slip away.

And then Mack-Dog learned: God sets us free in His love, Jesus makes the way through grace, and the Holy Spirit guides us home.

Time passes.

The boy says thoughtfully, "It's important to take some time to reflect on what truly matters to you—what you value most."

Mack-Dog wags his nub of a tail slowly, his eyes reflecting the sparkle of the stars above. A breeze gently rustles through the nearby grove of aspen trees. His heart whispers LOVE. *Without love, life is just a series of boxes. I want to be free.*

Not ready to reveal his innermost thoughts, he turns his head toward the boy. "And then what do I do with that?"

"You'll see." he answers, patting Mack-Dog's head.

Mack-Dog licks the boy's face.

He finds a comfortable curve of the hammock and falls asleep, rocking gently in the breeze.

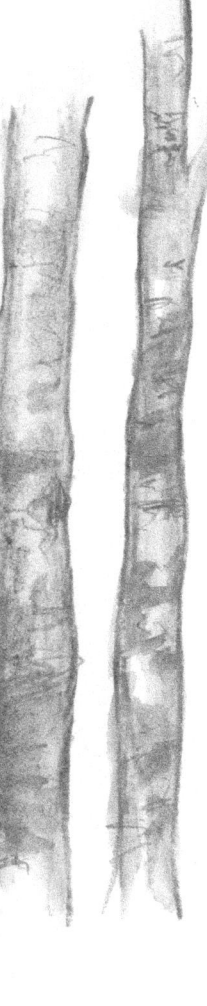

At sunrise, the boy senses warmth and feels the weight of a soft blanket resting over him. He rolls to his side, trying to remember when he moved from the hammock to the grass. He looks down next to him and sees a mug of coffee resting in the grass.

He watches a swirl of steam rise from the cup into the fresh mountain air.

He takes a sip, smiles contentedly, and says, "Mom."

Mack-Dog looks at him quizzically.

The boy looks into his companion's sleepy eyes. "Now you know what it feels like to be covered in prayer."

> And then Mack-Dog learned: Being prayed for wraps us in a love that never lets go.

REBUILDING TRUST

The days grow shorter. The aspens on the riverbanks change their colors to deep yellow as if trying to hang onto the final warmth of the summer sun.

One day Mack-Dog narrows his eyes and surveys the back porch. Something seems amiss.

Running shoes. Normal.

Fishing pole. Expected.

Cardboard box… cardboard box? Wait a minute.

The boy walks out the door, suitcase in one hand, backpack in the other. The door slams behind him.

Mack-Dog raises his head. He sniffs.

The boy sets down his backpack. "Summer's over," he says, scratching his dog's ears. "We're headed to the family ranch in Texas."

Mack-Dog nuzzles his friend's hand to encourage more scratching. He spies the open door of the pickup. He jumps in the front seat.

The boy places the backpack, suitcase, and cardboard box in the backseat of the truck. "Aren't you full of questions?"

Mack-Dog cocks his ears. "Not today."

And then Mack-Dog learned: Trust takes us to unknown places.

The rugged mountains of Colorado fill the pick-up's rearview mirror as the truck heads southeast.

Soon Mack-Dog looks out his window at the dry, flat ground filled with giant yucca and prickly pear cactus. He licks his front paw. "Why Texas?" he asks.

The boy lifts his cap and smooths his hair. "My great grandpa bought the ranch generations ago, and it's been handed down to our family. I was raised in Colorado, on the river, but we spend a lot of time at the ranch too. I love it there. I can't wait to show you the cows and the chickens."

The boy looks wistfully out the window. "I've always wanted to run the ranch for Dad, and now that I'm done with college and with our ranch hand retiring—well, it looks like I'll finally get my chance."

Satisfied, Mack-Dog stretches across the front seat with his feet in front of him and his butt in the air.

The boy realizes he's taking a curve too fast and breaks suddenly. Unable to keep his balance, his dog falls onto the floorboard.

They both begin to laugh.

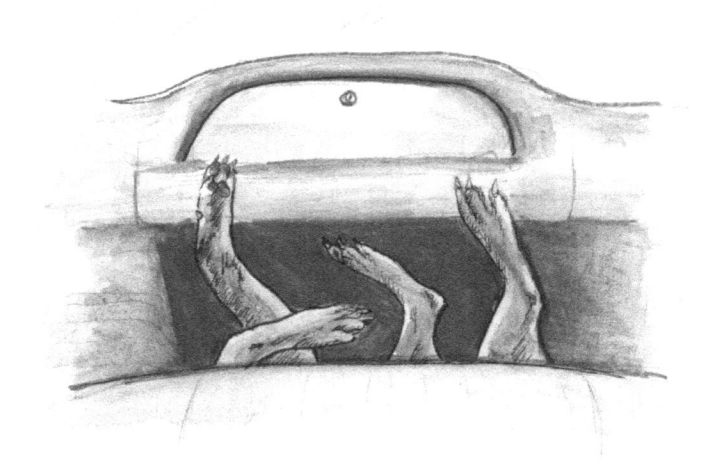

Mack-Dog stirs as the pick-up leaves the road and splashes across a shallow creek. Rocks grind under the weight of the tires. The boy rolls down his window, allowing the scent of cedar to fill the cab.

"A shortcut," he says with a grin. "We're almost there."

It's dark outside when the boy stops the truck and opens the gate. After he pulls through, he shuts off the motor and climbs out, inviting his friend to join him. Together, they walk to the back of the truck, where the boy lowers the tailgate. Mack-Dog jumps into the bed as his friend sits on the metal, his legs dangling over the edge.

The boy points to the stars. "Do you see it?" he asks.

Mack-Dog rests his head on the boy's shoulder and says, "The Big Dipper."

The boy puts his arm around his dog's neck. "God's here too. No matter where we are, He's there to guide us and invite us to follow His purpose."

Mack-Dog snuggles closer.

The boy lifts his cap and scratches his head. "It won't be easy here. There's a lot to do." He studies the constellation for a moment. "The ole' ranch hand kinda let things go when he decided to retire. And I gotta prove myself to dad."

Mack-Dog looks at the Big Dipper, unafraid.

> And then Mack-Dog learned: Healing asks us to believe God has a purpose, even when the path is difficult.

The sun peeks over the canyon. the boy sits on the porch, sipping his first coffee of the day. Mack-Dog stretches on his belly at his companion's feet.

Without warning, the peaceful morning is interrupted. A UTV speeds up the drive and spins a hundred-and-eighty-degree turn, barely missing the porch. Dust encircles the pair sitting on the porch. The driver tips his cowboy hat.

Mack-Dog walks protectively between the boy and the UTV. He spies a cow dog in the front seat—a blue heeler.

The boy stands and wipes a bead of sweat from the back of his neck. The blue heeler bares his teeth.

"The wife wants to give your mama some chickens to add to your brood. I'll catch the suckers and drop them off in the next couple days," the man says.

"That's very neighborly. Mom and Dad will be here in a few weeks, but Mack-Dog and I will take good care of them until then." He looks at the animal in the passenger seat. "New dog?" the boy asks.

"Yup. Named him Mud," the man says.

Mack-Dog cocks his ears from side to side. He narrows his eyes and studies the man. Then he looks at Mud in the passenger seat of the UTV. The rancher starts the vehicle and spins onto a cactus-lined road. As Mack-Dog watches the dust encircle the rig, he can't help feeling sorry for the Texas cow dog.

And then Mack-Dog learned: Staying guarded feels safe, but healing opens our hearts to others.

The boy walks back onto the porch and pulls on his boots.

Mack-Dog looks at him questioningly.

The boy hops into a UTV "Wanna go? Let's check on the chickens."

Mack-Dog scrambles into the passenger seat. After they arrive at the coop, the boy cuts the motor and sits quietly, studying the birds.

Mack-Dog eyes the flurry of activity in the pen surrounding the coop. "Now, what?"

"Based on those clucking noises, they're hungry."

"And then what?" Mack-Dog asks, giving his friend a long, side-eyed stare.

"We lock them up for the night," the boy says. He grabs a metal bucket filled with feed.

"I can't do that," Mack-Dog says. He jumps out of the UTV, turns away from the coop, and runs back to the ranch house alone.

An hour later, the boy rocks slowly back and forth on the porch swing with Mack-Dog at his feet. The soft glow of porch lights reflect a sense of contentment in the atmosphere.

Without warning, the chickens' clucking quickly turns to alarmed screeches. But the screeches aren't coming from the coop. Somehow, the chickens have gotten free.

Chaos erupts from the surrounding oaks, as a coyote slinks from tree to tree, looking for easy prey. Mack-Dog emits a low growl as he slowly creeps in the direction of the unwelcome predator.

The coyote trots toward a patch of giant prickly pear cactus. He runs toward the canyon as the full moon silhouettes the horizon, spotlighting the would-be thief.

The boy begins to imitate chicken sounds, trying to use his best bird-like voice. One by one the chickens timidly approach him. Lovingly, he picks up each bird and returns it to the coop. After he fastens the latch, he turns on the ball of his foot, looking at his dog with narrowed eyes.

"Do you know how they got out?"

Mack-Dog drops his head.

"Out with it."

The dog looks at his friend. "Can I hear your best chicken voice again?" he asks.

The boy hides a half smile. "The truth," he demands.

"I can't stand to see an animal locked away. It's scary not knowing when you'll be free." He paws the dirt. "I let them out."

"But letting them out put them in danger," The boy says, rubbing his friend's ears.

> And then Mack-Dog learned: It might feel natural to protect others from pain, but too much protection can cause its own kind of hurt.

After dinner, the two friends hop in the truck and take a ride through the oak brush and cedar canyons. Mack-Dog lays his head on Boy's thigh.

The boy pulls up to the ranch house. Before getting out of the truck, he lets out a sigh of contentment, soaking up the warm glow of the lights inside the house. Then he reaches for the door handle.

Suddenly the house goes dark.

The boy tenses, waiting for the light to return.

Mack-Dog hears some scratching sounds under the porch. The boy seems too worried about the lights to notice. Mack-Dog studies his friend closely. He sees something different about the boy. Mack-Dog scoots closer to his friend. "Are you afraid?" he asks.

"A little. I feel as though I need to take care of everyone, or everything will fall apart," the boy says. He finally opens the door of the truck.

And then Mack-Dog learned: Even our best friends have worries they may not know how to share with us.

"We should have electricity," the boy says. "Let's see why we don't." The two friends check the house and surrounding area. The boy reaches down and rubs Mack-Dog's ears for reassurance.

Mack-Dog searches his friend's eyes, still trying to understand what's different about the boy. Looking closer at his companion he asks, "What scares you?"

"Not being good enough. Letting people down." the boy looks at his boot.

Mack-Dog takes a closer look at the boy's eyes rimmed with shadows of stress. He blinks and looks again. He suddenly realizes what's different about his friend. There's something teetering on his shoulder.

It's a box.

And then Mack-Dog learned: Worry is sneaky—it packs our boxes with fear and pain until we're carrying more than we should.

As the pair sit on the porch, Mack-Dog's thoughts whirl in his head. The boy. The noise under the porch. The darkness.

Finally, a pick-up approaches the house. As it arrives, the headlights push back the darkness.

A rancher rolls down his window. "Hey kid, are you alright? All the electricity is out for a hundred miles. The crews are working on it."

Mack-Dog hears the boy's whispered sigh of relief.

While the boy and the neighbor talk, the dog watches his friend closely. He watches the box outline on his friend's shoulder fade in and out, eventually evaporating from sight.

PART III

Rediscovering Life

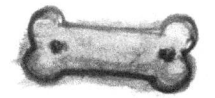

Mack-Dog returns to his morning post as the sun rises. He smells coffee brewing. He waits for the strange noises under the porch to start again.

He watches the gap beneath the porch. After several minutes, the nose of an armadillo peeks out, sniffing the air.

The armadillo catches a whiff of Mack-Dog and retreats to safety.

Mack-Dog shakes his head. He tries to understand all the new things he's beginning to see.

Several days later, the boy sits with his feet in the Nueces River. The gentle rush of the water tickles as it cools his skin.

The boy turns to his friend. "Hey, Pal, are you okay? Since the night we lost our lights, you've been quiet."

Mack-Dog looks away, not wanting to tell the boy what he saw that night.

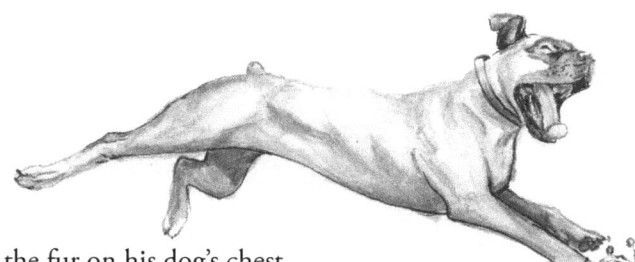

The boy roughs up the fur on his dog's chest.

Mack-Dog gives in to the reassuring touch. "I see things. Things I've never seen. Things that shouldn't be there."

The boy waits for his companion to go on.

"I see *boxes*. And they're everywhere. Yesterday, at the chicken coop, the cluckers were scared. The boxes sat right on top of their heads. Today, I watched an armadillo emerge from under the porch. A box rested on the tip of its nose. And whenever Mud comes around to bother me, an empty box swings from his tail."

He doesn't mention the box on the boy's shoulders.

The boy runs his fingers through his hair, weighing his next words. "It's okay," he says. "I see them too." He rubs the top of his head.

Mack-Dog sighs deeply. "What are they?" he asks.

"The hurts and fears we don't know how to heal on our own."

"What makes them go away?" Mack-Dog asks as he scratches his ear.

"Sometimes we just need someone to make us feel normal. Other times we need someone to guide us."

Mack-Dog cocks his head. "What can I do?"

"Love them. Sometimes, in the process, you'll start to see their boxes fade."

Mack-Dog jumps into the river with a gigantic splash and dances in the current. A plan begins to form in his mind as the cool water soothes him.

He feels needed again.

And then Mack-Dog learned: Feeling needed again doesn't mean we're fully healed, but it gently reminds us our story can offer comfort to others.

The boy pulls his UTV up to the front porch, relieved that the day's chores are complete. Unloading a sack of grain, he smiles to himself, thankful for the company of his trusted friend.

Mack-Dog leaves the boy's side and scampers behind the barn.

Without notice, a cloud of dust blows toward the boy. He shakes his head as he watches his neighbor and Mud speed up, eventually sliding to a halt as dirt rises around them.

Mack-Dog runs back to the boy and sits at his feet.

The rancher stands up as his dog bails out from the side of his vehicle. "Coming by with a warning. You better get prepared. Freak storm headed this way. Everything will be covered in ice tomorrow morning."

"What about the animals?"

"The livestock should be fine. It's the deer you need to worry about. It's hard for them to survive a cold snap like this." The man sticks his hands in his jean pockets and rocks back and forth on his battered cowboy boots.

The boy feels a pit in his stomach.

His guest continues. "A few years ago, we lost entire herds, and this storm is predicted to be worse. It's warm enough now, but just you wait." The rancher hoists a heavy leg into the driver's seat. "Now, where is my good-for-nothing dog?" he asks.

The boy looks at the barn. Both dogs emerge from around the back. Mack-Dog trots up to the boy, faking innocence.

Before jumping back into the UTV, Mud casts a covert glance at Mack-Dog. The rancher starts the motor. He whirls out of the drive.

The boy looks at Mack-Dog. "What are you two up to?" he asks.

His friend paws at the dirt. "What do you mean?"

"I've watched Mud's box hang from his tail since the rancher named him. You two disappear behind the barn, and now the box is fading."

"I showed him my secret stash of bones. They're all his now," Mack-Dog says, leaning into the boy's leg.

The boy waits for more explanation.

"He needs to believe someone likes him just the way he is. Now he knows I care about him more than my hidden pile of treats."

The boy studies the cloud of dust trailing the UTV. Mack-Dog follows his gaze.

And then Mack-Dog learned: When we believe we matter, we can give to others without running on empty.

Suddenly Mud emerges from the whirlwind of dirt following the UTV. He breaks into a run back toward the house.

The boy puts his hand on his hip. "What's this? He jumped out of the UTV." He looks again. "And he's carrying something in his mouth."

Mud runs up and lays a tennis ball at Mack-Dog's paws.

The boy smiles and picks up the ball. He pitches it into the sky as both dogs playfully race each other to retrieve it. Mack-Dog wins the race. The game continues. The dogs pant.

Eventually the boy rubs his shoulder. "Okay you two, it's time for chores."

Mud heads down the road where he left the rancher.

Mack-Dog runs to the first pasture to check for holes in the fence as the boy heads to the chicken coop to tuck the birds in for the night.

> And then Mack-Dog learned: Sometimes, just being there is enough. It's not the words that encourage healing, it's the love.

Mack-Dog finishes checking the last fence and heads back to the house. Walking the dusty road bordered by yucca, prickly pear, and barrel cactus, he notices a fawn curled up under a cedar tree. The baby watches the road expectantly.

The dog slows his pace. He turns toward the tree, tiptoeing through a cactus patch. The fawn briefly glances his way and returns her gaze to the empty pasture beyond the road.

Mack-Dog crouches as he crawls closer, careful not to rub his stomach across any stickers. He closes the distance between himself and the anxious creature.

She stands on wobbly legs, never taking her eyes off the open field. A circle of boxes hangs from her neck like a Hawaiian lei. Mack-Dog sits down just out of her reach. The fawn steps toward him. She snorts.

He snorts back.

The fawn takes a step closer and then playfully hops away, inviting Mack-Dog to chase her. With a wag of his tail, he bounds after her, weaving in and out of the cedar branches. They dart around the tree, changing directions, popping in and out, each trying to surprise the other.

Mack-Dog absorbs the fawn's boundless energy. Soon, they're both laughing in their own way. The fawn's high-pitched snorts encourage his playful barking. The worries and troubles of the day fade as they share a moment of joy.

Eventually, the fawn slows down. The play comes to a gentle stop. The dog catches his breath as he lock eyes with the deer. The gentle dog and the fawn sit side by side in the shade of the cedar.

The world around them seems to pause. In the arms of nature, surrounded by singing birds and the whisper of the wind, they find solace in belonging.

As his new friend curls up under the protection of the cedar, Mack-Dog watches over her until she falls asleep. He senses she's waiting for someone who may never show up. And yet, he can't ask her to leave.

He feels torn, wrestling between the fawn's vulnerability and his loyalty to the boy. Imagining his friend returning home to an empty house after finishing his chores, he steps onto the road leading home.

And then Mack-Dog learned: Love may tug us in different directions, but some bonds are never meant to be broken.

The next afternoon, Mack-Dog naps on the porch. The winter sun warms him, making him lazy. He rolls on his back, absorbing the heat. As he shifts his weight from side to side the porch boards leave an imprint on his back.

Suddenly, under the boards, he hears a scratch. The sound turns to clawing, gnawing, chewing, scampering, scurrying.

He scratches the weathered planks, mimicking the sounds below. He tips his ear toward the gap between the boards. He listens.

Nothing.

He starts the entire process again. He scratches. He waits. He hopes.

The board below his stomach softly vibrates as something claws the underside of the wood. He sticks his nose into the gap and sniffs.

Unexpectedly, a nose from below touches his. Surprised, he yelps. The nose waits for him to return.

"Hellooooo," Mack-Dog calls out.

The armadillo's nose twitches in response to Mack-Dog's greeting. She pokes her head up through the gap, her eyes meeting his with a mixture of fear and determination.

"Hey there," Mack-Dog says softly, trying to reassure her. "You're stuck, aren't you?"

The armored creature nods, her sharp claws scraping against the wood. "I'm looking for a safe place for my babies," she explains in a trembling voice.

Mack-Dog's heart begins to ache as he realizes the predicament the armadillo family is in. "I'll help you," he promises. "I'll find a way to get you all out of there."

"There's one problem." Mama Armadillo sighs. "And it's very embarrassing."

Mack-Dog leans in closer.

"I can't find my babies," she confesses.

Her potential rescuer looks at her quizzically, but he nods, encouraging her to continue.

"I can't tell you," she says, and the box on top of her nose grows. "No, no, no."

"I'm all you've got right now." Mack-Dog explains.

"Don't judge me." The box on her nose grows. "I'm so afraid the raccoons will find them; I keep digging tunnels. I can't stop. Now there are so many, I can't remember where I hid them."

Mack-Dog ponders Mama Armadillo's predicament for a moment.

Carefully, he sniffs the edges of the front porch. He identifies the scent of the armadillo babies coming from one of her tunnels, but he's too big to fit into the burrow. "I think this is where you need to look first. Make sure they're here before I start digging."

"That's it! I remember now," she says. "I piled a bunch of rocks at the entrance, so I wouldn't forget where I left them." She raises her nose in the air to look a little closer at her babies' rescuer.

"Mama, you wait right here," Mack-Dog instructs. "I'll dig down and get your babies out safely."

With focused determination, Mack-Dog begins to gently dig, taking care not to disturb the babies or cause any harm. After a few moments, he carefully uncovers the tiny baby armadillos curled up in their holes.

Mama Armadillo's eyes well up with tears of joy as she sees her little ones safe and sound. "Thank you, Mack-Dog. Thank you!" she exclaims gratefully.

Mack-Dog smiles warmly. "We're not done yet."

Meanwhile, the boy makes several trips with the UTV from the barn to several pastures preparing for the looming storm.

Darkness falls.

Finally, at the point of exhaustion, the boy sits on the weather-worn boards of the porch. He looks into the cracks. He puts his ear on the wood. "What did you do?"

Mack-Dog stretches his legs in front of him, raising his bottom into the air.

The boy presses. "Where's Mama Armadillo?" he asks.

Mack-Dog looks down at his paws. "Well, she has a new home."

The boy's half-grin encourages his friend to continue.

"She kept scratching and clawing trying to make her nest deeper with more tunnels. Her babies got lost in the maze."

The boy shakes his head. "Did you see her box?"

"Yeah, she needed a new start. I carried her closer to the river. She dug a new nest. Her family's safe."

The boy opens his arms to embrace his pal. "You're some dog. You know that?"

> And then Mack-Dog learned: When we're ready to rediscover what matters most, a little kindness and a fresh start go a long way.

The boy enters the house as sleet starts to fall. He is shaking and wet from buttoning up the ranch for the cold snap.

Mack-Dog playfully nips at his heels.

Together, they walk into the kitchen, and the boy starts a pot of coffee.

"Won't that keep you awake?" his companion asks, just starting to notice the boy's uncontrollable shivers.

"Not tonight. It's brutal on the UTV when it's this cold." The boy drains the warm liquid into a mug. He relishes his first sip.

Wanting attention, Mack-Dog leans into the boy's legs. Coffee sloshes out of the mug.

"Now look what you did!" the boy snaps. "Can't I have five minutes without someone needing something from me? Like I don't have enough to worry about right now?"

Mack-Dog presses his ears against his head, trying to shut out the hurtful words.

The boy walks into his bedroom and flicks out the lights.

Mack-Dog pads quietly to his place at the foot of the bed without a word.

Hours later, he senses the boy tossing and turning. "How's that coffee working for you now?" he asks.

The boy punches his pillow. "It's not the coffee."

Mack-Dog hops onto the bed. He nuzzles his friend's neck. He licks his ear. And then he sits on his chest.

"You gotta move," The boy says. "I can't breathe."

"Not until you apologize. And I can make things a lot worse." He turns and aims his tail at the boy's nose.

"Okay, okay. I'm sorry. I've been sorry for two hours. I just didn't want to say it." The boy playfully pushes Mack-Dog. "When we were in Colorado and Dad needed help down here, I thought I could handle this huge job on my own. Now the tanks are freezing. The cows are always hungry. And the dang chickens try to escape the coop every single day. To say nothing of the wildlife management."

The boy stretches his hand out to his friend. "It's too much. Maybe I'm not that brave or grown-up—even though I want to be."

Wanting to reassure the boy, Mack-Dog licks his face. "Everything will look better in the morning," he says and rolls into a ball next to Boy.

The exhausted ranch hand snuggles into his treasured dog, who waits for the boy's breathing to slow.

They fall asleep.

> And then Mack-Dog learned: True bravery comes when we're honest about what makes us feel small.

Hours later, the boy awakens, feeling bed sheets tangled around his feet, exposing his toes to the frigid air. He half opens his eyes. Realizing the absence of his buddy's body heat, he is suddenly alert. The empty room causes him to jump out of bed.

As he runs onto the porch, he slips and falls onto his back, a sheet of ice making it impossible to stand. Slowly and cautiously, he puts on his boots and heads toward the barn and the UTV. He senses something happened during the night.

He opens the barn door. His eyes begin to adjust to the darkness.

Hundreds of eyes stare back at him.

REDISCOVERING LIFE 73

He quietly enters the barn. He walks gently to the first stall.

Mack-Dog looks up at him. Next to him, a fawn nuzzles closer for protection.

The boy backs up, not wanting to frighten the baby. "Why?" he asks.

"Her mother never returned," Mack-Dog says. "I found her under a cedar tree. When the sleet started last night, her herd was searching for protection. She led them back to me."

As the boy's eyes adjust to the darkness, he sees hundreds of deer staring back at him. Their eyes shine. Their breath turns into vapor in the cold air.

Overwhelmed, the boy falls to his knees. His trusted friend saved hundreds of animals as the rest of the world slept.

He murmurs. "I didn't have to fix it all myself."

And then Mack-Dog learned: We don't have to do it all alone. Sometimes, help is just waiting to be welcomed in.

The next day, the sun melts the ice from the storm. Animals emerge from hiding places. Birds begin to sing.

The boy enters the barn. All the deer are gone.

Well, all but one.

The boy walks to the first stall. Mack-Dog looks up at him, reminded of the first time the boy opened a door to a box he didn't know how to leave.

The boy reaches down and scratches behind his friend's ears. "It's time, Pal."

Mack-Dog licks the fawn's face. "I know."

The boy feels a river of love escape from the corners of his eyes. It runs down his cheeks, dripping off his chin.

His friend looks at him with eyes reflecting a new vulnerability. He stands. The baby beside him takes a tentative step forward. Together, they walk out of the stall and leave the barn.

Mack-Dog senses a shadow to his right. He investigates the underbrush. He noses the baby toward the cedar bush. The lead doe waits on the other side.

The boy follows his companion's glance and nods.

And then Mack-Dog learned:
Love knows when to embrace and when to let go, because love trusts that what belongs to you will find its way home.

PART IV

Risking Love Again

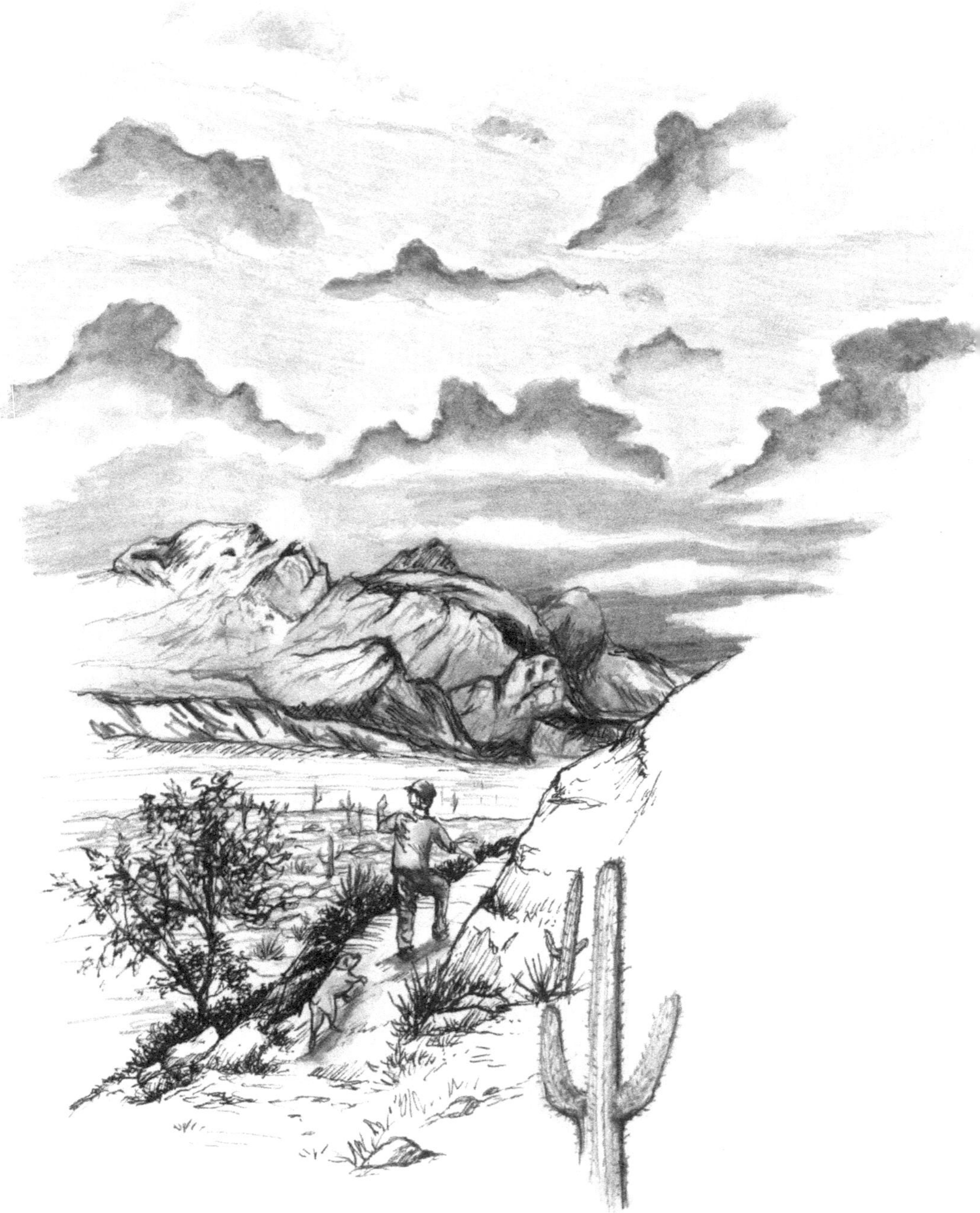

A couple days later, the boy runs his finger along Mack-Dog's collar. "Hop in the UTV" he says.

The boy drives as far as the vehicle will go along the trail. The setting sun illuminates a series of hills, forming a recognizable shape. He smiles at his furry friend.

Mack-Dog whines softly.

The boy tenderly strokes the dog's head. "Teddy Bear Mountain," he says. "Do you see his feet and his rounded belly?" He points to the highest peak. "And there's his nose."

Mack-Dog solemnly scans the horizon and nods in agreement. "What are we doing here? It's still a little icy."

The boy starts up the trail, carrying a backpack filled with blankets. "When you climb a big hill, you can see all the amazing stuff from the top—even if it was difficult to get there."

Silently, the pair climb over rocks and through the scrub.

When they reach the top, the boy spreads out the blankets and pats the soft spot beside him. Mack-Dog settles in.

"What do you do when it hurts?" Mack-Dog whines. "This loving and helping stuff made me feel good at first, but right now, I'm just empty."

The boy rubs the dog's shoulders. "When my heart's depleted, I climb Teddy Bear Mountain. See the Big Dipper?"

Mack-Dog nods, trusting his friend's wisdom.

"I can't fill up on my own. There is only one source that will fill my soul. And that is Jesus. He is the only One who never runs dry. His love and grace overflow even the Big Dipper. When we surrender to His purposes, we experience the life He promises."

Mack-Dog stretches out on his stomach and places his head between his paws, feeling a new fullness in his heart.

"Why do you try to fix everything by yourself?" Mack-Dog asks.

The boy stretches his hands over his head. "I haven't found her."

"Her?" Mack-Dog asks, moving closer. "You mean I'm not enough?"

"There is only one you. We're a great team and that will never change." He strokes the top of his friend's nose. "But we need her to keep us soft."

"How will you know when you find her?"

The boy concentrates on the Big Dipper as if whispering a silent prayer. "She'll smell like yellow roses."

Mack-Dog shakes his head. "Yellow doesn't smell."

"But when I pray for her, in my mind I can't see anything else."

The two friends watch the crescent moon emerge from behind a small cloud, each lost in his own thoughts—the boy hoping he finds her soon.

> And then Mack-Dog learned: Sometimes, the heart's deepest needs are met in quiet prayers while waiting for what's meant to be.

As the Texas sun rises the next day, the boy tosses his duffel bag into the bed of his pick-up truck.

It's time to go home to Colorado.

Mack-Dog stands by the passenger door. He holds a tennis ball in his mouth.

Mud runs toward the truck, ready to play. the boy throws the ball as the two friends chase one another, laughing and biting at each other's heels. Their game continues until both dogs run toward a bucket of water and take a drink.

Eventually, it's time to go. Mack-Dog drops the frayed tennis ball at Mud's feet. He pushes it with his nose, encouraging his companion to keep the ball that brought them so much joy.

Mud rolls his gift back to Mack-Dog. "I want you to keep it, so you don't forget me."

> And then Mack-Dog learned: Distance doesn't change our love for our friends.

Mack-Dog watches out the back window as the ranch fades into a cloud of dust. The boy rolls his truck windows down. A warm breeze washes through the cab. The radio plays classic country tunes, blending with the rhythmic hum of the engine. Mack-Dog rides shotgun. Occasionally, he leans out the window, savoring the scents of the open road.

After a while, he curls up in a tight ball with his head resting against the boy's thigh. Pretending to sleep, he thinks about everything he learned on the ranch. He feels restless.

He's ready to return to the river.

He sits up and wipes a string of drool onto the boy's jeans. Distractedly his friend wipes it away with the back of his hand.

Mack-Dog softly nips at the boy's ear.

"What's gotten into you? Are you getting sentimental?" the boy asks with a grin.

Mack-Dog laughs it off. But he can't shake the shadow of worry creeping into his thoughts.

I know he feels alone, Mack-Dog thinks. *But what if he finds her, and she replaces me?*

And then Mack-Dog learned: Fear whispers that love might run out, but real love doesn't dwindle or expire.

Eventually they make a pit stop for sweet tea and fuel. A giant sign covers the gas pumps. Closed for Annual Art Walk.

The boy groans and pulls out of the station. He makes a wrong turn.

"Well, Mack-Dog. Looks like we're headed into town." He impatiently drums his fingers on the steering wheel. "Let's stop. Maybe they'll have a food truck or two."

In the heart of the dusty town, the annual art walk transforms Main Street. The boy sips on a cold drink, thankful for the companionship of his dog. They wander aimlessly as a bluegrass band adds to the atmosphere.

Pop-up galleries line the sidewalk, each hosting local artists engrossed in their work. As the evening sun dips low, the boy loses himself in the atmosphere, feeling the weight of responsibility begin to fade. He looks down, expecting to see his trusted friend at his side.

He's gone.

The boy gasps. He whistles. Nothing.

He starts to panic. Moments of frustration turn into fear. *Where is he?*

The boy whistles again.

Mack-Dog eventually emerges from the crowd.

The boy breaks into a run. "Where were you?" he asks.

His companion sits at his feet.

"And why is there a spot of yellow paint on your nose?"

Mack-Dog circles behind the boy, nipping at his heels.

"Are you in trouble? If you crashed into someone and made a mess, we need to leave."

Mack-Dog bites his heels harder. The boy glares at him. Mack-Dog runs in front of him leading him way through the crowd.

The boy follows. He spies his dog sitting next to a large easel. The boy's heart skips a beat. All he can see are the artist's legs below the painting. Then the artist steps to the side of the painting as if evaluating it. The boy's curiosity intensifies.

And then Mack-Dog learned: Trust can mean taking a risk, even when you're not sure what comes next.

The artist peeks out from behind her canvas, pallet in one hand, paintbrush in the other. She smiles like she expects him to be there. "Your dog?" she asks.

The boy looks down at the top of his shoe. "Um, yeah."

A drop of paint falls from the tip of her brush.

Mack-Dog turns in circles. The artist and the boy start to laugh.

Shyly, the boy steps a little closer. He glances at the back of the canvas. "Can I look?"

She reloads her brush, picking up a dab of paint from her pallet. She studies the dog. "Okay," she says.

He steps around the canvas, trying not to trip on the legs of the easel.

Mack-Dog looks at him expectantly.

The boy quietly draws in a breath. He tugs on his ear. He smiles. "What are you going to call it?"

The artist looks from the canvas to the dog and then at the boy. "The Yellow Rose of Texas, what else?"

One Year Later...

After returning from their Hawaiian honeymoon, the couple could barely contain their excitement. Could life get any better?

Trusting brown eyes gaze at them—trying to trust, anyway. The week he'd spent with the boy's parents had been full of a nervous tummy and interrupted sleep. Would history repeat itself?

The artist rubs Mack-Dog's ears. She buries her face in his fur. "Come on Pal, follow me," she says.

Mack-Dog hesitates as she opens the door to the bedroom. The boy stands proudly at the foot of the bed. He points to a smaller one on the floor.

The artist kneels and takes Mack-Dog's face in her hands. "We made a commitment to God and to each other. To love, honor, and cherish each other no matter what life brings."

The boy kneels next to his wife. "And our promise includes you, too. We're a family now."

For the first time Mack-Dog understands that that life can indeed begin again. Sure, it might be different than it was at the beginning.

It might even be better.

That night, the presence of love lulls Mack-Dog to sleep.

He finally knows what it feels like to be whole.

> And then Mack-Dog learned: We can go through really hard things, and still find our happily ever after.

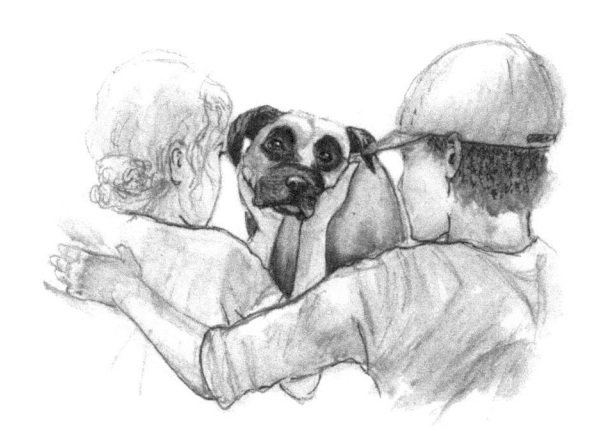

A Final Note from the Author

Dear Precious Soul,

When a certain friend of mine really loves a book, she refuses to read the last four pages because she's not ready to say goodbye.

I would be honored if you are hesitating to shut the back cover. This tells me that you may not be ready for our beautiful healing journey to end. You are on your way, but you're not alone.

There may be days when something reminds you, we live in a world that

- Pushes us to go it alone.
- Tries to put our healing on a timeline.
- Makes it difficult to trust again after we've felt abandoned.

It's during these times I hope you will open this book again. Draw in it. Color the pictures. Write in meaningful Scriptures. Make it a reflection of what you've learned.

You will heal.

You don't have to earn it. To prove it. To bargain for it.

Healing doesn't have to feel like being tossed around in a current that's too strong to handle. Through these pages, you've discovered how to move with the process in a way that doesn't leave you overwhelmed but leaves you softer, stronger, and more at peace.

You are ready to love again.

Before you go—here's one last gentle discovery I made while writing this story for you: *True healing is only possible with the acceptance of God's grace.* It isn't something you have to hustle for, something that everyone **else** deserves.

Grace. A gift. Freely given by God. No strings attached.

And it's for you.

Love,

Dani

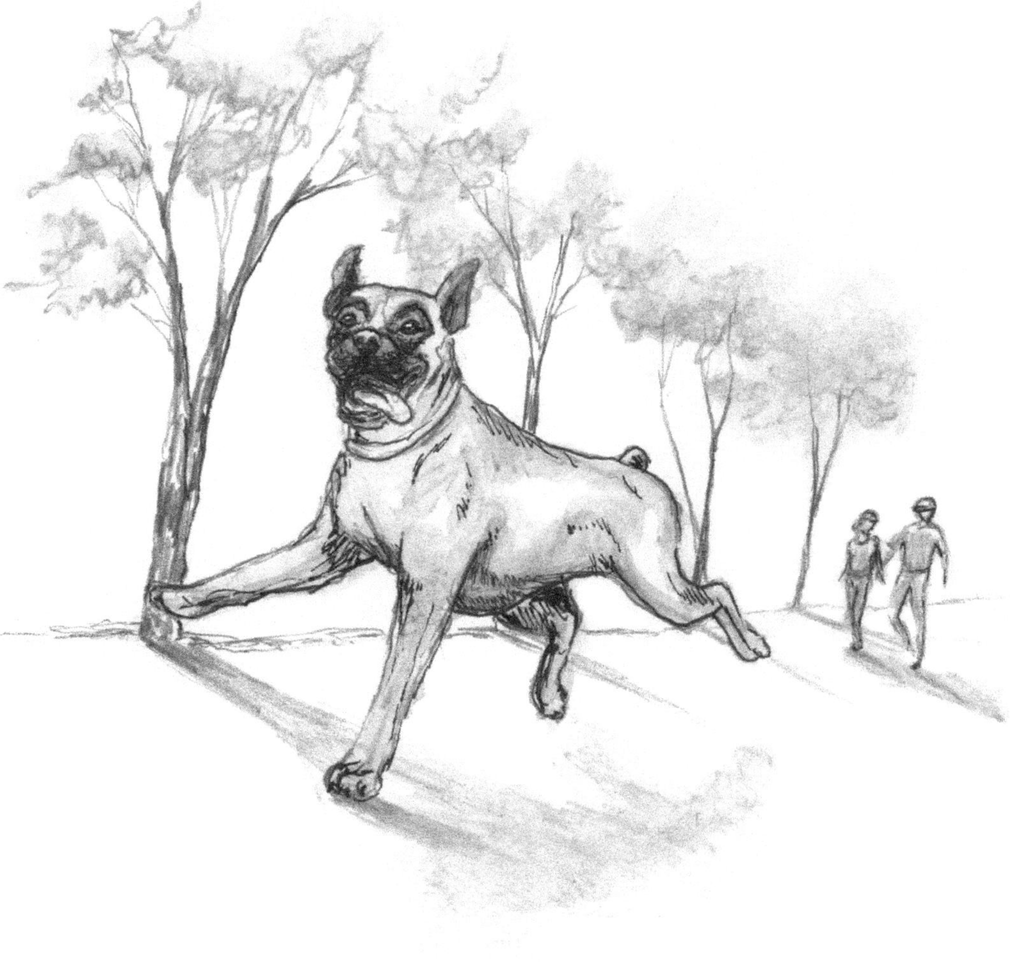

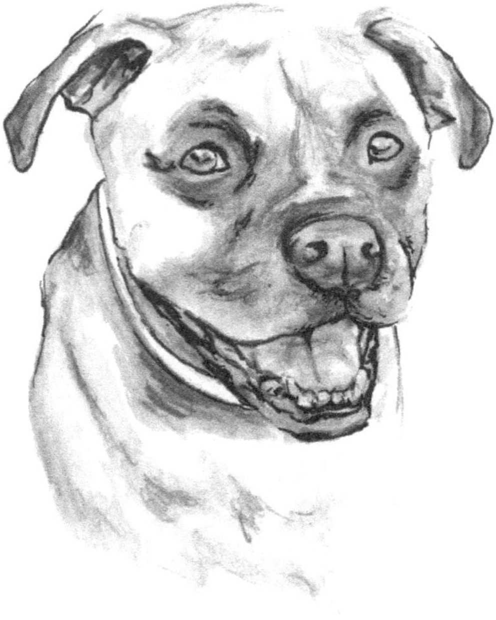

Acknowledgements

To my husband, Michael—my life truly began when I married you. You have been my greatest support, my anchor, and my encourager. You taught me the importance of faith, adventure, and believing in myself. Time and again, I've come to you with new dreams, and never once have you told me I wasn't capable. Instead, you've been the steady voice reminding me that I can, and you've done everything in your power to make sure my dreams come true. I am endlessly grateful for you. And remember, *I love you more.*

To my four Js—Joey, Jason, Justin, and Jordan—thank you for showing me that life is an adventure, a journey, and a gift. No matter what challenges have come our way, our family has stood firm in faith, and because of that, we've shared an incredible life together. Now, as I watch you step into the next generation, building families of your own, I am in awe of the beautiful legacy God creates through love.

Justin, you've had a front-row seat to this creative process on both sides—living it with me during the day at work and watching Jenna bring it to life through her illustrations. You've posed, adjusted, and made sure every detail looked just right. But more than that, you were the inspiration for this story. Seeing the way you care, the way you believe in people, and the way you loved an abandoned dog—it all made its way onto these pages.

And to Jordan, my Jiminy Cricket, you have a way of illuminating the path with your wisdom, kindness, and unwavering love. Everyone needs that one person who speaks truth with gentleness, who reminds them of who they are and where they're going—you've been that for me.

Finally, to my brother. Your kind heart and caring spirit go before me and guide me.

To my writing family—I could not have done this without you. First, to Illumify Media, thank you for believing in me and putting in the hard work behind the scenes to bring this book to life. From the very beginning, you have been a team I could trust, and I am so grateful for your dedication.

A special thank you to Cheri Gregory, my writing coach. Your wisdom has helped me understand the heart of writing—not just words on a page, but real people, real stories, and real challenges.

To Susie Eller, thank you for starting me on this journey, and to Karen Bouchard, who believed in me from the first moment I walked into a writing conference—I will never forget your encouragement.

Betsy St. Amant—fiction editor, teacher, and the one who instilled in me a deep appreciation for the true em dash, the rhythm of action beats in dialogue, and the sweetness woven into every story.

Angela Bouma—my brilliant web designer, who turns ideas into beauty and always greets me with a cheerful *Hey, friend!* in every email.

Tonya Kubo—the marketing whiz who showed me that marketing isn't just about strategy; it's about caring for people in creative, joyful ways. And yes, you made social media fun.

To my friends who have walked this road with me—Debi Moore, Marla Larson, Amy Engelman, Shannan Cloud, and Kim Haar—thank you for being my sounding boards, my encouragers, and the ones who weren't afraid to say, "Try something different." Your support has meant the world to me, and I know you're celebrating with me today.

Finally, to the many friends I've been blessed with—whether from Africa, Scotland, or across the United States—you have been part of this journey in ways big and small. You are my tour bus companions, my prayer warriors, my encouragers, and my joy. I hope you know how deeply I treasure each of you.

God has truly blessed me, and I am forever grateful.

35 Lessons from a Mended Soul

Step by step, hope nudges us forward.................................Page 16
Hard things don't change who we are, but they can make us forget for a little while..................................Page 17
When it comes to healing, the path forward can hold unexpected twists. ....Page 20
We often give to others what we long to receive ourselves. ....Page 22
Even during the loneliest moments, love is revealed in the way we care..................................Page 25
Sometimes the path home doesn't feel fair, even when it's taking us to where we long to be. ....Page 26
Even when fear makes a mess of things, real love doesn't walk away. ....Page 29
When we feel like we don't have all the answers, it's okay to return to a place that feels safe..................................Page 31
Sometimes pushing a little is a way of asking, "Will you forgive me?"..................................Page 32
Sometimes kindness finds its way back to us in the most unexpected ways..................................Page 33
Letting go feels safer when we know a true friend will always be there for us. ....Page 34
We try so hard to be perfect, but real love isn't something we have to earn..................................Page 41
We need to be patient with ourselves as we become who we really are. ....Page 42
Stepping forward means gently releasing the past and letting hope lead. ....Page 43
God sets us free in His love, Jesus makes the way through grace, and the Holy Spirit guides us home. ....Page 44
Being prayed for wraps us in a love that never lets go. ... .Page 46

Trust takes us to unknown places. ....*Page 47*

Healing asks us to believe God has a purpose, even when the path is difficult. ....*Page 49*

Staying guarded feels safe, but healing opens our hearts to others. ....*Page 50*

It might feel natural to protect others from pain, but too much protection can cause its own kind of hurt. ....*Page 53*

Even our best friends have worries they may not know how to share with us. ....*Page 54*

Worry is sneaky—it packs our boxes with fear and pain until we're carrying more than we should. ....*Page 55*

Feeling needed again doesn't mean we're completely healed, but it gently reminds us our story can offer comfort to others. ....*Page 59*

When we believe we matter, we can give to others without running on empty. ....*Page 61*

Sometimes, just being there is enough. It's not the words that encourage healing, it's the love. ....*Page 62*

Love may tug us in different directions, but some bonds are never meant to be broken. ....*Page 64*

When we're ready to rediscover what matters most, a little kindness and a fresh start go a long way. ....*Page 69*

True bravery comes when we're honest about what makes us feel small. ....*Page 71*

We don't have to do it all alone. Sometimes, help is just waiting to be welcomed in. ....*Page 73*

Love knows when to embrace and when to let go, because love trusts that what belongs to you will find its way home. ....*Page 74*

Sometimes, the heart's deepest needs are met in quiet prayers while waiting for what's meant to be. ....*Page 78*

Distance doesn't change our love for our friends. ....*Page 79*

Fear whispers that love might run out, but real love doesn't dwindle or expire. ....*Page 80*

Trust can mean taking a risk, even when you're not sure what comes next. ....Page 82

We can go through really hard things and still find our happily ever after. ....Page 91

About the Artist

The thoughtful, expressive style of Jenna Grosse brings stories to life in a way that speaks to the heart.

A Colorado based artist and illustrator, Jenna works in many art mediums and styles, and is particularly talented in oil, acrylic and graphite realism.

A principal theme in Jenna's art is the living world. When she was a child, Jenna's passion for horseback riding inspired her to start painting. Learning how to paint the anatomy and biomechanics of equine movement was the beginning, and before long she was expanding her repertoire to include nature scenes and wildlife. Today, her deep affection for nature and the peace it brings continues to inspire every piece of art that she creates.

Jenna holds a Bachelor of Fine Arts and has exhibited in various galleries across the U.S. She loves spending time with her husband, being a mother, and enjoying the company of her horses and cats.

An invitation from Jenna:

If you love the artwork in The Boy, the Boxer, and the Yellow Rose and are interested in commissioning a piece or discussing book illustrations, I would love to hear from you! Please reach out to me at: jennaleigh.art@gmail.com.

About the Author

In a world where helpers often give until they have nothing left, Danielle Grosse offers a different path forward filled with grace, self-compassion, and a renewed sense of purpose. Through her writing and ministry, Danielle helps others reconnect with the Heart of a Helper—the tender space of empathy and love—without falling into exhaustion or obligation. She speaks to individuals who have carried too much for too long, teaching them how to let God and others pour into their empty hearts so they can give from a place of true sweetness, rather than sheer duty.

Danielle's passion for healing is rooted in personal experience and deep professional training. She is completing her certification as a Certified Mental Health First Responder through the American Association of Christian Counselors and has received specialized training in spiritual care for the sick and dying through Hospivision and the University of Pretoria in South Africa. Her background uniquely equips her to guide others through the delicate balance of helping others while staying whole.

When she's not filling the world with words, Danielle is out exploring it. Alongside her husband, Michael, she can be found bumping down roads less traveled, always seeking stories of resilience, grace, and the quiet strength of those who choose to love anyway.

An invitation from Danielle:
I love sharing encouragement, behind-the scenes glimpses of my creative projects, and updates on upcoming speaking events. If you'd like to hear from me, I'd like to stay in touch!

Visit my website: https://daniellegrosse.com
Send me an email at danielle@daniellegrosse.com
Find me on Facebook: https://www.facebook.com/danielle.grosse.7
And remember: We're in this together, and I'd be honored to walk this journey with you!